Fun in the Sun

by Bobby Lynn Maslen
pictures by John R. Maslen

Scholastic Inc.
New York • Toronto • London • Auckland • Sydney • Mexico City • New Delhi • Hong Kong • Buenos Aires

Available Bob Books®:

Set 1: Beginning Readers

Set 2: Advancing Beginners

Set 3: Word Families

Set 4: Complex Words

Set 5: Long Vowels

Ask for Bob Books at your local bookstore, or visit www.bobbooks.com.

ISBN 0-439-14499-X

6 5 4 3 2 10 11 12 13 14

Printed in China 68
This edition first printing, May 2006

The sun was hot.

Pop had a top hat.

Mom had a red wig.

Peg had a big cap.

Pop got the red wig.

Mom got the big cap.

Peg got the top hat.

Mom, Pop, and Peg sat
in the sun.

Mom was OK.

Peg was OK.

Pop was hot!

Pop, Mom, and Peg had fun in the hot sun.

The End

List of 22 words in Fun in the Sun

Short Vowels

Aa	Ee	Ii	Oo	Uu	sight
and	end	big	got	fun	a
cap	Peg	in	hot	sun	OK
had	red	wig	Mom		the
hat			Pop		was
sat			top		